Crisis at Lake Sharue

Crisis at Lake Sharue

Johnny E. Ware II

Copyright

Printed in the United States of America

First Printing, 2017

ISBN-13: 978-1-942022-65-7

The Butterfly Typeface Publishing
PO BOX 56193
Little Rock, Arkansas 72215

to mankind …

Preface

Crisis at Lake Sharue is an animated story of morality and teamwork. This fish community of diverse species is suddenly faced with a crisis that requires them to come together to conquer a common issue of concern, that could very well end their existence.

Although they had a representative for each species, they chose one leader that would ultimately represent the best interest of all species best interest. The leader only reacted when he had the whole groups support for each individual crisis and communicated effectively with everyone during times of concern.

In the history of mankind, it has often been demonstrated that during difficult times, people are able to put aside their differences for the common good.

This story reminds us of our heritage and natural inclination towards helping each other. Our world is in a crisis of sorts now. Will the human race follow the example set by the community of Lake Sharue?

It is my hope that we will indeed follow the Lake Sharue family and continue to live in harmony forever!

-Johnny E. Ware II

Once upon a time, there was a fresh water lake somewhere in America called Lake Sharue. Lake Sharue was considered to be one of the most beautiful lakes in the world.

The lake was far away from cities in a secluded area of the country. The lake had a very happy community of different wildlife and a few different species of fish such as catfish, bass, crappie and brim and plenty species of bait fish such as skipjacks, shad and minnows.

The leader of the lake community was a catfish called Captain Whiskers. Captain Whiskers was elected by the community to be in charge of safety and the clean water act.

Each lake species has one representative for each group. For example, Captain Whiskers represented the catfish and all other species, Sargent Speck represented the crappie, Quick Strike represented the bass, and Sun Spot represented the brim.

Johnny E. Ware II

The four representatives met five days a week in the early mornings to discuss the day's business or any concerns the citizens may have often discussed, such as security, clean up detail, and how to respond to different emergencies.

During the emergencies the alarm was sounded by a snail called Slow Stuff. Slow Stuff used his shell to sound as the horn.

One morning before the morning meeting Captain Whiskers was doing his normal parameter check around the lake. While completing his check he had plastic bottles and trash that he found floating on top of the water.

Captain Whiskers took the necessary time it took to clean it all up. Finding all these pollutants were indeed a big worry to Captain Whiskers so he took his concern to the morning meeting.

Captain Whiskers was a bit late for the meeting because of all the trash he had collected. As the captain arrives to the meeting the bass Quick Strike said to Captain Whiskers, "Why are you late Captain?"

Johnny E. Ware II

Captain Whiskers replies, "I'm concerned. It's been almost twenty years since I have seen trash in our lake."

"I know what's going on," Quick Strike, the bass, replied. "As I feed in the shallows I've noticed humans here and around. They're around our lake having picnics and fishing for us mostly on the north end of the lake. In fact I've seen more humans around our lake in the last six months than I have in twenty years."

"You should have shared that information with us in our morning meetings," Captain Whiskers replied.

"I didn't think it was a big deal at the time." Quick Strike said.

Captain Whisker's replied, "Everyone, keep your eyes open!"

The weeks went on as normal with everyone doing their part as citizens, collecting trash, delivering mail and administrative duties.

On this particular day, a loud horn sounded and it was obviously the emergency call from Slow Stuff, the snail.

Naturally all the citizens of Lake Sharue assembled at town square to look for their representative to explain the emergency. The only rep that arrived to the square was Sargent Speck, the crappie rep.

So Sargent Speck had to become the spoke person for all species. All species were forced to come together as one group to find out what the emergency was and to find Captain Whiskers, Sun Spot, and Quick Strike.

Sargent Speck took charge and divided all the different species up by divisions to search all areas of the lake.

Sargent Speck, aware of all species characteristics, knew this time of year the bass and brim population spent more time in the shallows feeding. So he had them search the shallows.

Sargent Speck also knew that his species, the crappies, and Captain Whisker's species, the catfish performed better in deeper water this time of year. So he had these two divisions searching the deep waters of the lake.

A few hours later the search continues. The emergency alarm is sounded again by Slow Stuff. Everyone responded by being organized and civilized. They returned to the town square to find Captain Whiskers, Sun Spot, and Quick Strike with sad expressions on their faces.

Captain Whiskers shouts out to the crowd that had already arrived, "Citizens the time has come for our community to face some issues and we will discuss them in ten to fifteen minutes once everyone has arrived."

Once everyone arrived, Captain Whiskers called Sargent Speck, Sun Spot and Quick Strike to a small circle and whispered to the three reps for about five additional minutes.

The crowd was starting to get agitated and impatient. Captain Whiskers looked up at the crowd and said, "Citizens of Lake Sharue, as your chief security officer and your clean water act administrator, I have no comfort in telling you that the north end of our lake home is being classified as unsafe and unlivable."

The quiet one, Sun Spot, shouted, "Cut the short talk Captain Whiskers. Tell us what's wrong?"

Captain Whiskers cleared his throat, "Um, um, um," and then he said, "We've discovered that the north end of our lake home has become polluted by humans.

There is virtually no oxygen because of the waste and chemical runoff. Some humans are aware of the harm that they are causing, but there are some that are hurting the environment and are completely unaware.

We also know why the bait fish are so plentiful on our end of the lake. The bait food such as shad, skip jack, and minnows cannot survive in a low oxygen environment just like our species."

Sargent Speck shouted out, "Captain, what the heck are we going to do?"

"Settle down, Sargent Speck," the captain replied.

"Now I know why I got so tired while trying to feed on the north end shallows, low oxygen and no food," Quick Strike revealed.

"We're having our normal meeting tomorrow morning," Captain Whiskers assured them, "to discuss our plan of action."

Slow Stuff shouts out, "When will you guys share the plan with us?"

"Right after our meeting," Captain Whiskers responded. "I will inform you to sound the alarm for the lake community meeting right here at town square."

"I need each of you reps including myself," Captain continued, "to select some of your top guns, species from your individual groups to be on lookout for tonight and throughout tomorrow morning."

Johnny E. Ware II

The night continued as normal while most of Lake Sharue's community slept except the group selected to stay on watch and patrol throughout the night.

Then about 4:00am, before everyone had awaken, the emergency alarm sounded louder than ever.

Everyone was quite startled and wondered why the alarm sounded so early. They slowly headed towards the town square.

Captain Whiskers and Slow Stuff were the first to arrive, but the rest of the community continue to appear in slowly as if the alarm wasn't as important as it once was.

Captain Whiskers shouted out angrily, "Slow Stuff sound the alarm once again!" With a sense of urgency Slow Stuff did just that.

After Slow Stuff blew the emergency horn the second time, it almost sent the community into panic mode, but it got them there quick.

Johnny E. Ware II

Captain Whiskers turned towards the crowd and cleared his throat to create silence throughout the square. Just as Captain Whiskers opened his mouth to speak a loud vibration rumbled through the water. Then seconds after that, a strong shockwave came through with physical force and knocked everyone off their tails.

Captain Whiskers quickly returned to the standup position and stated, "Citizens of Lake Sharue, I am getting straight to the point! This morning Slow Stuff and myself were doing a perimeter check and we heard machine-like noises while we were at the north end of the lake.

We proceeded to the surface to get a good look at what was making those sounds. As we got closer to the surface we realized it was harder to get oxygen on our gills because of the low oxygen supply.

When we finally reached the surface our eyes could not understand what we were seeing because of the oil that existed. Humans were everywhere with long convoys of bull dozers, tractors and trucks."

Slow Stuff shouted out, "We also know what made the shock wave that just knocked us off our tails. It's as if they were trying to drain our lake or something."

Captain Whiskers said, "I don't think so, but we will have to come up with a plan of action."

"If they're not draining our lake, they are probably building homes around us." Quick Strike suggested.

Sun Spot shouts out loud, "You know that's bad news!"

Captain Whiskers replies, "Sun Spot I hope you are wrong and if you are right we will positively deal with any issue's that confronts us."

"After we dismiss," the Captain continued, "I would like the reps, Sargent Speck, Quick Strike and Sun Spot, to go and meet with each individual group and discuss different ideals and strategies to deal with different emergencies. Afterwards, the group leaders and myself will meet again at 3:00pm to discuss all of your individual group ideals."

Sargent Speck replies, "I've got some ideals now Captain!

"It would not be fair to your species, crappie, if they didn't have an opportunity to voice their opinions," said the Captain. "Everyone should be involved in this decision."

"Citizens' of Lake Sharue," the Captain pleaded, "Please understand how serious this issue can become. Take this time to meet with your individual group so we can evaluate your ideals for this issue of concern. Please sincerely debate different ideals and thoughts that each of you may have.

I will meet with my group, the catfish, and get their ideals and thoughts. Then I am going to the ancestor archives of emergencies to see if there's any information that might be beneficial to us during this crisis.

As I stated earlier, I will meet with the reps at 3:00pm and then at 7:00pm, we will all meet here again at the town square. Thank you for your cooperation."

At 2:00pm Captain Whiskers had conducted the meeting with his fellow catfish, and was now about to descend to the ancient log of knowledge, where he studied different strategies from the ancestor's emergency archives.

Upon leaving the secret waters, the Captain decided to take a quick lap around the lake before meeting with the reps at 3:00pm.

As the Captain arrived on the north end of the lake, he was able to confirm what caused the shockwave earlier. It was the trees hitting the water as they were being cut down, some at the same time which caused the shock wave. The humans were clearing the land for some type of development!

Captain Whiskers arrived back to town square a few minutes before his scheduled meeting with the reps. All the reps were already there waiting on the him.

Quick Strike was quite excited and quickly responded by letting it be known that he had some great ideals from his individual group.

"I'm sure you all have great ideas so let's get started with the meeting," the captain said. "So let's begin the meeting. First I'm going to share some information with you reps, before I give the floor to you all. As I did the perimeter check before this meeting I want to tell you what I observed. There is extensive construction going on, on the north end. There are trees in the water and trash and oil from the machines.

I also confirmed the trees hitting the water simultaneously is what caused the shockwave we experienced earlier. The humans are already clearing the land for some type of infrastructure.

Sadly, I also noticed a few of our citizens that did not listen and adhere to our warning about the lack of oxygen, which has caused them to lose their lives.

In fact, once our meeting is over we must send a rescue party out to retrieve their bodies for their families."

The reps all grew solemn.

Sun Spot said what everyone was thinking, "Does it not amaze you guys that before this crisis occurred, we were not always respectful to each other."

Johnny E. Ware II

They all hung their heads in shame.

"As a brim, I know from experience Captain that sometimes in the past your species, the catfish, would sometimes eat us and Sargent Specks family, the crappie, and Quick Strikes' family, the bass." Sun Spot continued.

Captain Whiskers responded quickly, "If you want to be 100% truthful Sun Spot, Quick Strikes' family, the bass, have been known to eat my family the catfish, Sargent Specks family, the crappie, and really feast on Sun Spots family, the brim. We could go on and on about this issue because nature has a way of making things happen for a reason.

Remember when all our species got sick and 50% of us died. If it had not been for my family, the catfish, none of us would have survived. We catfish were designed to eat all the pollutants and diseased species of the lake and it not harm us."

"Over population in our environment and disease were the only times that this issue occurred," the

Captain continued. "The important thing to remember now is that we've come together when we needed to in order to conquer this issue before us."

Everyone nodded in agreement.

"Tell us about your group's suggestions and ideals," Captain Whiskers encouraged Sun Spot who was known to be soft spoken.

"My group's ideals are pretty simple, but effective," Sun Spot began. "We believe that all species should observe what we are eating, don't eat the bait humans put out for us, and avoid the nets they may put in the water. By the humans not being able to catch us it would discourage them and they would leave."

Captain Whiskers replies, "Thank you Sun Spot for your efforts and ideals. We will discuss every groups plan after all groups have spoken."

Next Captain Whiskers spoke to Quick Strike. "Quick Strike let's hear what your group has discussed."

"Thanks Captain," Quick Strike replied. "If you've noticed I've been pretty quiet up to this point in the meeting. My species, the bass, just somehow wants to move to another lake because we do not think we can stand up to the humans. Some humans conquer, kill, and destroy and we want no part in that."

Some of the group nodded again in agreement.

Quick Strike continued to speak, "Sometimes through carelessness they throw trash in our water that choke our young ones and they allow chemicals from their pesticides and weed killer residue to flow in our lake when it rains.

After they have contaminated the land, we can only sit by and watch them contaminate our environment. I wish I knew one human who cared enough to stand up for us and our environment. They don't realize that our species and other species live in their drinking water."

Captain shook his head and replied, "Thank you Quick Strike for those legitimate words and concerns. Now it's time for us to hear from Sargent Speck group."

As Sargent Speck rose to speak, another shock wave rushed through the water and everything and everyone standing either shook drastically or fell to the bottom.

Once the water settled down, the citizens headed towards the town square quickly, without hearing an alarm.

Sargent Speck rose to speak, "Fellow citizens, my species, the crappie, are really spooky and really don't want to deal with the humans. If my species had a choice we'd probably just stay deep until all danger has passed, so we will go with whatever the majority decides."

The town square has now filled with all the citizens of Lake Sharue. Captain Whiskers takes his turn to speak, "Yes, citizens of Lake Sharue, our situation is becoming more dangerous by the minute. I have already met with my group, the catfish, and everyone from my species is telling me to do whatever is best for *all* species.

Some of you know after the meeting with my species, the catfish, I went down to the ancient log of knowledge and searched through the ancestor's archives of emergencies in the deepest part of our lake.

The vibe that I'm getting from you all is that you want me to make the decision on how we will respond. There was indeed one point in the archives that I know would help us out in this particular situation. This act is secret and will not be discussed with anyone."

Then Slow Stuff shouts, "Whatever you are going to do, I would suggest you hurry and do so. Look at everyone's eyes and the expressions on their faces. I didn't even sound the alarm, yet everyone arrived quickly this time! The humans are now putting stuff down on the ground to make roads call asphalt right where they cut down trees."

Sargent adds, "Captain we believe in you and we know you have all of our best interest in mind."

"Captain," Sargent Speck continued. "Just go down to the log of knowledge and do whatever the ancestor's archives of emergency direct you to do."

That's when the crowd shouts in unison, "Hip, hip, hurray, hip, hip, hurray."

"I am preparing as I speak to descend to the log of knowledge," Captain Whiskers said. "I want to prepare you all for some changes that may occur after my descent to the deep.

You must not panic, everything will be alright. The water clarity most likely will change, pressure will increase, there probably will be a strong current and the bait fish will not be as thick on our end as they have been for a while.

Other things may occur, but don't be alarmed. Make sure our young understand the possibilities before the event occurs. I will return tomorrow night or the next morning.

Upon my return, I will have Slow Stuff sound the alarm to have a town square meeting to inform you of our status. I'm leaving Sargent Speck in charge until I return. As I leave you I would like to say thank you for your cooperation and dedication during this crisis. See ya soon!"

And with that, he was gone.

Johnny E. Ware II

The next couple days came and went with no word from Captain Whiskers. Sargent Speck and Quick Strike were doing the normal perimeter checks and noticed around the edges of the lake that the water was really muddy and they could not see out of the water.

"Sargent, have you noticed how the pressure has even changed?" Quick Strike broke their silence. "Look, there's bait fish back on this end of the lake and there's a good oxygen supply on our gills."

"You're absolutely correct, Sargent," Quick Strike agreed. "And did you notice that it took a bit longer to reach the surface? We're fighting currents and you know my species, the crappie, do not like strong currents."

"Wait one moment", said Sargent Speck, "Captain Whiskers told us about these potential conditions. Let's head back and get a crew to form a search for the Captain."

As Quick Strike and Sargent Speck began to head back to town square to form a search party,

Sargent Speck notices a dark figure several feet ahead.

Sargent Speck speaks, "Look Quick Strike that looks like a school of bait fish. Let's go and check it out. Whatever that is the closer we get to it the smaller the dark spot gets."

Sargent Speck recognizing the object was moving, so he says, "Halt, who goes there?"

Whatever the object is it doesn't respond, but continues to get closer.

Quick Strike says, "It's not a human, is it?"

"No," said Sargent Speck.

Sargent Speck calls out again, "Halt, who goes there?"

Suddenly, a voice cries out, "It is only I, my citizens."

Sargent Speck replies, "Captain Whiskers, is that you?"

"Indeed it is," replies the Captain.

"Fish, it is good to see you!" Quick Strike says with relief.

Captain replies, "It's good to see you all too!"

Captain Whiskers continues to speak as they head back to the town square, "Hey Slow Stuff, sound the alarm so we can have a town square meeting."

"Captain we were really beginning to worry about you," Quick Stuff states, "We noticed all the things you had mentioned before you left that could occur while you were gone, did occur, as you can see. The water got cloudy and deeper."

"What exactly did you do Captain?" Sargent Speck asked.

Captain Whiskers responds, "Sargent Speck you know that's secret information and there's only a few things I can share with you. I will have more information during our meeting. It's only been ten minutes since Slow Stuff sounded the alarm so let's give the citizens another ten minutes."

Johnny E. Ware II

Captain Whiskers recognizes the town square is now filled with Lake Sharue citizens. The Captain speaks, "My fellow citizens of Lake Sharue, I have never been so proud to stand before you and tell you that the issues of concern that once haunted us and our way of life is no more. That's right citizens, I said no more! Our ancestors have come through for us once again through the ancestor's emergency archives."

"What exactly did you do Captain Whiskers?" Slow Stuff yells out.

"Slow Stuff, unfortunately all of the information listed in the ancient archives is secret and cannot be discussed with anyone," Captain Whiskers replies. "I can tell you about some of the results and how it will impact our lives. I'm sure you've noticed that the pressure has changed and it takes longer to reach the surface. We have gained exactly one mile in diameter in every direction of our lake. The north end of the lake where the humans cut down the trees are now 25 to 30 feet under water and the humans moved all of their equipment before the flood. Now where they cut trees we can use for shelter. We've got forest in the lake which increases our insect diet and oxygen supply."

Quick Strike says, "Captain with all due respect, what makes you think the humans will give up now?"

"Quick Strike, I think the humans will give up because it will be at least another fifteen or twenty years before the water even starts to decline because the landscape once held water before," the Captain replies and then goes on to say, "Citizens I must say, with all the emotional distress that we've gone through as a community, I'm proud of the fact that even though we are all different species and not all alike, we were able to come together to make a difference and to achieve a common goal."

Sun Spot shouts out, "Do you think humans will ever be able to come together? What amazes me is that they are the same species, yet some hate simply because of color. Maybe humans need to experience something catastrophic like we did in order to come together as we have. "

The community all agree that the humans should take a lesson from them.

However Quick Strike isn't convinced it can be done. "I don't think they can commit themselves as we have."

Captain Whiskers has the final word, "May our community thrive for many years to come. I wish to all a good life."

The End

About the Author

Johnny E. Ware II is an Arkansas native. This is his second book. An avid fisherman, lover of history and writer, Mr. Ware hopes that his writings are perceived as a beacon for people to come together during extreme odds to defeat the crisis of life by supporting each other and using moral standards.

The Butterfly Typeface Publishing House Co.

The Butterfly Typeface Publishing House Company is a full service professional publishing company. Our goal is to 'spread a message' of inspiration, imagination and intrigue in all that we do.

Whether you hire us to edit, ghostwrite, publish (books & magazines) or web design, you can be guaranteed exemplary customer service, fairness and quality.

Our vision, under God's leadership, is to serve and assist in the healing of the heart, mind and soul of *all* people we encounter with integrity, intentional influence and positive purpose.

"We make good GREAT!"

Iris M. Williams – Owner
The Butterfly Typeface Publishing House Co
Little Rock Arkansas

www.butterflytypeface.com

www.ingramcontent.com/pod-product-compliance
Lightning Source LLC
Chambersburg PA
CBHW071226170626
46809CB00005BA/1958

* 9 7 8 1 9 4 2 0 2 2 6 5 7 *